OPALS FOR HOPE

BY

R J KALPANA

BEJEWELLED FAMILY SAGA
BOOK - 2

Opals For Hope (Fiction/Novel)
Copyright © R. J. Kalpana Ph.D 2020

First Published - May 2020

Published by –Pen & Ink Solutions, Chennai - 600090
Contact: penandinksolutions@gmail.com

This novel is a work of fiction. Any resemblance to actual persons, living or dead is purely coincidental.

All rights reserved. No part of this publication may be reproduced, stored in or introduced into a retrieval system or transmitted in any form or by any means (electrical, mechanical, photocopying, recording or otherwise) without the prior permission of the publisher. Any person who does any unauthorised act in relation to this publication may be liable to criminal prosecution and civil claims for damages.

Cover Image - Georges van den Bos

OPALS FOR HOPE

October's child is born for woe
And life's vicissitudes must know
But lay an opal on her breast
And hope will lull those woes to rest

The fabled eastern gems of the Bejewelled One, the Queen's jewels are more cherished than gold and more valued than life itself. It is said that only the worthiest may behold them for they are promised riches and happiness beyond dreams.

EPISTLE

Your most exalted Person, your Grace, Duke of Andover,

Salutations your Grace! I pray this missive of mine finds you safe.

The fear of intruding too far on the honour of your Grace and the fear for your Grace's life has kept me silent thus long.

I was transported with joy on receiving your letter and went down on my knees to thank god that you are alive and well.

I know your prudent regard has forbidden you to put words on paper but I well understand the constraints of communication and fear that it might fall into evil hands and thus endanger your gracious self.

After long reflection and much deliberation I will leave the important occurrences in London to be transmitted to your Grace by abler hands.

I shall only acquaint your Grace of much

awaited news that is within my knowledge and unknown to others.

After searching most diligently, I have finally been able to find a cottage to your exact specifications, your Grace. It goes by the name, Opaline, a whimsical name for sure.

I shall furnish the location upon your arrival in London. And I pray it suits your requirements.

I have refrained from making contact for fear that it might trigger an ambush for I am as much in hiding as we all are.

It is time to come home, your Grace. And so it will begin all over again!

I remain yours most humble and obedient servant,

Timms

PROLOGUE

The sound of screaming and death cries below started penetrating the walls of the castle. The children huddled together wondering what was happening. Soon they will know. Soon they will make a decision that will change their lives forever. Soon they will part forever.

The nursery door flung open and their elder brother, Dominic, ran into the room with a sword in his hand. He skidded to a stop in front of them and took a moment to look at them.

"My beloved sisters and brothers" Dominic said tearfully. "The Graces, the Duke and Duchess, mama and papa..." his voice broke but he swallowed the tears and continued manfully, "They are dead and the Rajah's men are coming after us now."

There were screams and tears all around him until he lifted his hand and silence once again filled the room as his brothers and sisters looked on with bravely but with tears coursing down their cheeks.

"We will fight them" said Wulfric. His second

brother as he stepped forward with fists clenched. Mr. Timms protested.

Dominic once again lifted his hand and stopped the flow of words as his sisters and brothers all agreed to fight.

"The fight will be for another day. This I promise you. Mama and Papa's death will not go avenged. We will not rest until the land is stained with the Rajah's blood."

They all nodded solemnly.

"But today we are not prepared. Today we must part ways and hide. It will confuse the Rajah and his men for they will not know where to find us. As long as we are alive, even one of us, we will avenge their deaths."

"Will they come for us?" asked Sita crying.

"Yes they will. We have the Queen's Jewels. The Rajah covets them and he must have them at any cost. Remember the story mama and papa told us about how papa helped mama escape from India…"

"And they fell in love and mama stayed on in England" finished Leila.

"Yes but the Queen's Jewels are mama's heritage and the Rajah sought to steal from her."

"We will not give it to them" tumbled the determined words around him.

"No! We will not!" agreed Dominic. "But for now, go and be safe. Stay alive! At any cost!"

They promised they will stay alive at any cost clutching the Queen's Jewels in their childish palms.

They gathered the nursemaids and footmen and told them exactly what must be done. Timms instructed them where to go and whom to meet and how soon to contact.

Then Dominic took over. He solemnly kissed each of his brother and sister and pressed their own gems into their hands and made them and their guards swear to keep them safe.

"I will come for you" he promised solemnly. "Then we will be together again. One family."

With this promise ringing in their ears, the children parted ways and escaped from the castle Andover through its secret passages known only to the family.

They ran confident that their elder brother will come for them and that they only have to hang on long enough for him to make everything safe for them to be together once again.

CHAPTER ONE

She came awake with a start, her heart pounding, her mouth dry. She looked wildly around her clutching her dagger in her hand. Slowly her eyes focused onto the frilly curtains on the window, the low cross-beams on the ceiling.

She remembered where she was and who she was. She slipped from the bed and made her way in the dark to the corner of the room and slowly slipped down and sat cross-legged on the square rug that was placed there.

With trembling hands she found the match and struck a light and slowly lit the oil lamp. The light flared in the dark and in its hue one could see a painting of a smiling couple and a painting of a blue-coloured man with a flute.

She sat in silence with tears flowing down her cheeks and slowly brought her breath under control. She closed her eyes and let the peace wash over her as the dawn slowly arrived flowing gently into her room.

The sun felt warm on her face, the light breeze carried with it the promise of the scents of budding flowers and fresh green grass. Finally, she turned her head and witnessed the sparrows and larks flitting among the branches of the tree just outside her window. Even that and their chirping songs failed to warm her cold heart.

She sat watched the painting in front of her, her parents, remembering the smiles, the laughter, the warmth, the love. "I miss you both" she said to the silent couple in the painting. "You were taken far too soon. What am I to do without you?"

She wiped the single tear that tracked down her face, sniffing. Her clear yet lightly coloured blue eyes scanned the cloudless sky, absently wondering if her parents were up there somewhere, watching over her.

"I pray that is so. You are out there in a special place, still looking out for me. I wonder where the others, my brothers and sisters are, I pray they are safe. I pray Dominic is safe and will come for me one day."

The sound of a horse interrupted her thoughts and her privacy and she turned once again to look out of the window wondering who would be visiting her so early in the morning. It was mid-morning by the look of the sun in the sky.

The horse stopped at the gate of her little cottage and Squire Grimes climbed down and made his way to the front door.

She sighed and got up to go down to the front room to greet the nauseating man. She couldn't afford to offend him.

Her bedroom opened up to a tiny landing with a flight of narrow stairs taking her downstairs into the tiny front room. She reached downstairs just as the knock sounded on the front door.

She opened the door and saw Squire Grimes smile at her, "Good morning, Mrs Mallory."

"Good morning, sir," Sita offered him a polite greeting.

She disliked him with his narrow face and calculating gaze still she smiled politely as her mother taught her.

"This visit is unexpected," Sita commented. "What can I do for you?"

Squire Grimes smiled leeringly at her and said, "It's not proper for a young thing like yourself to be alone in this world, so I have come to offer my protection."

Sita looked at him in shock, "I wasn't aware I was in need of any protection."

"You are now alone in the world, Mrs Mallory," replied Squire Grimes easily. "You have no one to look after your best interests. Your parents are dead and so is your husband."

Sita stifled the urge to laugh in his face. "I assure you, sir, I have no need for anyone to look after my best interests. I do thank you for your concern however."

For a brief moment, something ugly marred his face and Sita stiffened upon seeing it. Then it was gone and Squire Grimes smiled again.

"There are people who are less than gentlemen and they will prey upon you. I would like to offer my protection so you will be saved from all such unwanted attentions."

Sita's polite smile vanished as did her humour, "I have no interest in coming under your protection, Squire Grimes."

"You may wish to reconsider that," he said smoothly. "The world is a harsh place for a woman alone."

"That might be so but even that will not tempt me to come to you for help," snapped Sita.

"I do hope you are not making a mistake, my dear. Think of the joys of the marital bed. You must be missing it so."

"Squire Grimes! That's enough, sir."

"I have influence and you would do well to reconsider."

"Is that a threat?"

"It is what you make of it," he replied his voice smooth. "Women after all are the property of men."

"So you consider me as property? Well, this property is well able to take care of herself."

"That is your mistake," Squire Grimes lips thinned.

Sita shrugged "It's mine to make, isn't it?"

"I will give you time to reconsider, my dear. I will come to you tonight."

He turned and pulled open the door and walked out of the cottage and got on to his horse and galloped away.

Sita stared stunned at what just occurred. She hurried back inside the house and started packing.

An hour later, her maid, Martha, walked in with fresh eggs and milk from the local farmer, "My lady," she called.

"In here, Martha," she sang from her bedroom.

"My lady! What are you doing?" asked a shocked Martha as she saw the clothes strewn across the bed and a portmanteau open on the floor beside the bed.

"Oh Martha!" cried Sita throwing herself in Martha's arms.

"There! There! Child" patted Martha. "Tell me all about it."

"That odious man was here," Sita sniffed.

"Squire Grimes?" Martha asked.

Sita nodded.

"What did he want this time?"

"Martha, he offered me his protection and the pleasures of the marital bed."

"Good lord! That worm!" exclaimed a shocked Martha.

"We did decide that I should be a widow," reminded Sita.

"I thought widowhood was protection enough," said Martha sheepishly. "Now, what are we to do?"

"He said he will come to me tonight."

Martha gasped loudly. "No wonder you are packing. And rightly. We have to leave now."

"But Martha," protested Sita. "What about your wages from the big house?"

"I got an advance," confided Martha.

"However did you manage that?" asked Sita curiously.

"I heard there was a fair coming to the nearby village and thought to take you there," confessed Martha.

"Oh Martha! You are a dear," said Sita and hugged her maid.

"Oh go on!" said Martha laughing. "Never mind the fair now. We won't have time for that."

Sita's face fell. "No, we won't," she said softly.

"I am sorry child," said Martha saddened by the pale face of her charge.

"It's alright Martha," said Sita smiling. "This is not the first time this has happened and I doubt if it's the last. Come, let's away. We don't have much time if we have to put distance between this place and ourselves."

"Yes, let's finish packing and move on."

"Where will we go this time Martha?" asked Sita in despair.

"We will think of something child, don't you worry," encouraged Martha.

Together they finished packing and took the little gig and soon were on their way away from the cottage and the estate.

The cottage lane turned left onto the country lane and was empty of traffic. Soon they were trotting smartly away and Sita heaved a silent sigh of relief.

"Milady, I have been thinking," said Martha hesitantly. "Have you given thoughts to marrying anyone?"

"Martha!" exclaimed a shocked Sita.

"Now milady," begged Martha. "Hear me out first. It has been twelve years since we escaped from Castle Andover. I don't know where the others are and his Grace hasn't seen fit to visit us in all this time."

"Martha!" protested Sita. "Dominic might be in danger. He would have come if it was safe."

"May be so milady," agreed Martha. "All I am saying is time is a running and you ain't getting any younger. This is the fifth time in so many months that we had to run."

"I am so sorry, Martha," said Sita apologetically. "You should settle down somewhere and let me go on my own."

Martha snorted. "Much good that will do. For you don't know a thing, milady, begging your pardon."

"It is way too late for me Martha," said Sita sadly.

"You are beautiful enough to catch a young man's eye, milady and you should pass on your good looks and that rich golden hair and stunning figure to your children."

"There is more to marriage than just genes, Martha. There is love."

"You will be loved milady. I have no doubt," said Martha confidently.

"It's too late for that Martha," said Sita quietly. "Not the kind of love mama and papa had."

"Ah, my dear, theirs was a rare love, envied by man and god alike," said Martha sadly. "Perhaps if you would just settle for someone who is kind to you."

Sita sat silently staring at the road ahead refusing to let her tears fall from wet eyes, refusing to let her dreams die.

CHAPTER TWO

They took the back roads leaving the main road for stagecoaches and post-chaises so they will be away from curious eyes. They stopped at an out of the way inn and had a little luncheon and continued on their way.

They were still traveling as the moon peeked through the trees and rose high up in the sky. It was only when it reached its zenith that they stopped awhile.

Sita tiredly looked at the boundary wall of a huge estate hugging the road and noticed that they had just arrived at its rickety gate.

"Martha?" she asked questioningly.

"We have to stop now milady," said Martha. "The horse is tired and so are we. I am thinking we have put enough distance between Squire Grimes and ourselves and it is time to rest."

"There is no inn here Martha," said Sita pointing out the obvious.

"No milady but this is an estate, isn't it?

Bound to find work here."

"Oh Martha!" cried Sita. "The trouble I am to you. You should have left me and gone a long time ago and made your own life."

"Nonsense milady," snorted Martha. "I gave my word I will look after you. And after we lost the Queen's Jewel, there was no way I could let you stay on your own."

"Oh Martha! Whatever will mama and papa say? They will be so disappointed. And Dominic will be furious."

"No, milady," said Martha gently patting Sita on her back. "If I know your mama, she would be glad that you lost the jewel but stayed alive. And as for Dominic, he would not be the boy I knew if he becomes furious with you now."

"I miss him," sighed Sita. "I miss them all and wonder where they are now."

"Come milady, get you some rest now, while I go and check out the house," said Martha laying down a quilt on the gig and fluffing a pillow.

Sita stood up. "No Martha! This time I am coming with you."

"But milady!" protested Martha.

"The least I can do is accompany you. And I will be quiet, I promise"

Martha sighed and nodded. "Alright then, come this way and make no noise mind!"

They slowly made their way in the moonlight

through the rickety gate that wasn't latched and which sprung open when pushed. They exchanged surprised glances but made their way down the long driveway with its overgrown grass.

"Doesn't look like there is anyone living here Martha," whispered Sita.

"Hush! We don't know yet, just look at the window," said Martha as she pointed to the distant second floor window which stood open and inviting with a flicking light.

They crawled up to the grand house which lay sprawled indolently dominating the countryside and would have been awe-inspiring if it was well-maintained. As it was it had a tumbledown appearance and looked ghostly in its ruins.

They stopped for a moment and looked up. The window was open as it had been for the past hour while they made their way through the tall grass closer to the building.

"Do you think someone is in residence?" asked Sita worriedly.

"Someone must have lit that lamp," whispered Martha. "Although…there is something very odd here."

"What is it?"

"There are no lights in the main part of the house."

"Which means?"

"Come, let's go back to the domestic quarters

where the servants are," decided Martha and started her way to the back of the house. Sita followed her obediently.

They made it to the back of the house quietly with nary a rustle and Martha peeked once through the lit window to see a man and a woman sitting down to a large dinner. Her mouth watered at the chicken roast and vegetables but she ducked her head and pulled Sita hurriedly away from the there.

"The servants are in there having their dinner," whispered Martha hurriedly. "But there are only two of them."

"What do we do now?"

"We will see who is there on the second floor and then we can decide on a plan," said Martha.

"Alright" nodded Sita resignedly and sat down on the grass to remove her shoes.

"What are you doing milady?" asked a shocked Martha.

"I am removing my shoes, Martha," said Sita matter-of-factly. "How else am I to climb up to the second floor?"

"But milady…" protested Martha.

"Hush! You cannot climb two stories, so how else are we to know who is there?" asked Sita reasonably looking at her maid in the moonlight.

Martha looked worried as she chewed her lips.

"Come, Martha, I will be fine," promised Sita. "Think how many trees I have climbed and how many windows I have climbed out of."

"That may be so milady," said Martha primly. "But this...I don't like it."

"Shhh" said Sita standing up and gazing at the window above her. Clouds drifted by in the night sky riding on a light breeze leaving the stars to twinkle brightly on their own. The moon playing peekaboo with the clouds cast shifting shadows. Perfect conditions, she thought.

She placed her hand on the drainpipe. It was old and rusty in places. She prayed it would hold on until she got to the top. She threw Martha a smile and a wave and climbed onto the pipe like a monkey.

Soon she was swinging her way to the top. She reached the first floor and edged her way along the windows until she reached the place where the back of the building met the side wall. Now she only had to balance walk on the ledge until she reached the side which would place her directly under the lit window.

Luckily her feet were narrow and she had excellent balance. Mama taught her how to balance on her toes, on her heels as she practiced the Classical Court dances with her sisters and brothers laughing at each other as they fell and ran out of breath and went dizzy with all that pirouetting.

Then papa would come and sweep mama up

laughing and carry her up the staircase to the ducal chambers.

Sita sighed and swept a tear from her cheek. She set out across the ledge. She could sense Martha hovering below but she ignored her. Steady now, one foot after the other. Easy now, a few more steps and she jumped, clung to the wall, scrabbling at the stone until her hand came in contact with the drain pipe.

She heaved a sigh. Now the rest was easy. She was right beside the open window on the second floor. She leaned into the window and listened. Not a sound could be heard. She looked in and could make out a bedchamber.

A four-poster bed, heavy hangings around the bed, an ornate wardrobe, a dressing table with a lit candle but there was no sign of life.

She swung one leg over the sill as she pulled herself up and then she was in tumbling onto the carpet. She crouched a moment in the darkness awaiting sounds of discovery. She waited for her eyes to adjust in the gloom breathing deeply to let her racing heart slow down.

CHAPTER THREE

"**H**ave you come to steal from me?" a hoarse whisper stirred the darkness and nearly stopped Sita's heart. She swung around, scanning the room for someone, anyone, bracing herself to flee.

Nothing moved, not even the shadows. There was no sign of anyone Sita thought puzzled.

"I asked if you have come to burglar me?" came the whisper irritated this time rather than frightened.

It came from the bed.

Sita narrowed her eyes.

"Of course not!" she replied indignantly forgetting to whisper.

She tiptoed closer to the bed, straining her eyes in the darkness. What she had taken initially as a bundle of clothes thrown on the bed was actually an old woman lying awkwardly. Her nightclothes twisted into a bunch.

Sita waited quietly seeing if the old woman

would scream or try to raise an alarm. For if she did then she would be gone faster than the old woman could take a breath.

"You are not here to kill me?" the old woman asked.

"No," replied Sita shocked.

"You are not here to burglar me?"

"No."

"Then why are you here?"

"I..." Sita bit her lip. She didn't discuss with Martha what was the story they were going to tell now. So she floundered helplessly.

"I doubt there is anything left here for you to steal," said the old lady tiredly.

By now, Sita's eyes adjusted to the gloom. The old woman was right.

The furniture was old and heavy and thick with dust. There was nothing in the room worth stealing, no silver knick-knacks, no paintings on the wall, no strings of jewellery. Nothing.

It was a sorry excuse for a room in such a grand mansion, Sita thought sadly. From outside the house had looked quite grand, ancient but grand and inside it just reeked of neglect and disrepair.

Although...Sita sniffed delicately. What was that smell?

The old woman stank. Good lord! There was no one looking after her. Clearly she was bedridden but to leave her in such a condition. Sita was furious.

"May I have some water?" croaked the old lady.

"Of course" said Sita and filled a glass from a jug on the side table.

The old lady reached for it, her hand trembling, old and withered as it was.

"Here, let me help you," said Sita and slid an arm beneath the old woman's shoulders and propped her up so she could drink, holding the glass to her lips. She was all bones and skin.

The old woman drank thirstily, the whole glassful.

"Thank you," she said weakly. "I needed that."

Sita smoothed the pillows and tugged the bedclothes and straightened her nightclothes into a more comfortable arrangement. She finally settled the old woman to her satisfaction and stood back in silence.

"Odd sort of burglar you are," said the old woman watching her.

Sita refilled the glass with water and set it closer to the old woman and removed the tea tray out of sight. The tray contained a bowl of something dried and disgusting no doubt.

She sniffed her nose delicately.

"Gruel!" snorted the old woman. "That's all I get these days."

"How long has it been here?" asked Sita.

"Since this morning."

"Who brings you food?" Sita asked curiously.

The old lady laughed "The servants. Got to keep me alive else they won't get paid."

"You have servants?" Sita asked in disbelief as she cast a glance around her.

She silently glided to the door and peered out into the corridor. It was dark but in the faint moonlight she could make out the floor was thick with dust.

She crept down the corridor and looked through every room on that floor and stopped at the staircase. All were the same: dusty, neglected, unused.

There couldn't be servants. Nobody has cleaned here for months.

She returned to the old lady's bedchamber and said, "You cannot have servants. The place is filthy."

"A sorry excuse for servants but I do have them," nodded the old lady suddenly tired.

Sita suddenly remembered what Martha said has she looked through the downstairs back window into the servant quarters.

"Well, there might be servants, incompetent ones, no doubt. I will take my leave Mrs…"

The old lady held out her hand in a courtly

gesture, "I am Lady Clara Beddington, my dear. How do you do?"

Sita took the old lady's hand and curtsied gracefully, "A pleasure to meet you my lady but I cannot tell you my name," she said regretfully.

"Perfectly understandable, my dear. So what are you going to do now?"

"Do?" For a moment Sita couldn't think what she meant.

"Well, you didn't climb through my window just to hand me a glass of water now, did you?" said Lady Clara shrewdly.

"Oh that...I don't know," floundered Sita helplessly.

"You weren't born to this life, my dear. You weren't taught to curtsy like that if you weren't born in the highest echelons of Society and you have the accent of a lady."

Sita bit her lip before she revealed herself.

"Are you desperate? Fallen into hard times?"

Sita shrugged. She wasn't going to admit anything or explain anything for there lay a road fraught with danger. Lady Clara might be old and incapacitated but she was very sharp and shrewd.

"Lady Clara, I have to leave now," she whispered desperately. "Is there anyone I can inform to contact you? The Doctor perhaps?"

"I have no family dear," Lady Clara shrugged. "Just a nephew who left for India ten years ago and I am yet to hear from him."

Sita's heart jumped at hearing the word India but she contained it and asked politely, "Friends then?"

"I haven't had a caller in...forever, I guess," said Lady Clara tiredly. "Everyone's forgotten me."

A sliver of moonlight caught the gleam of a tear as it slowly slid down a withered dirty cheek.

"I don't need anyone. I am fine," she said fiercely.

Sita didn't bother to contradict her.

It was obvious to the both of them that Lady Clara was far from fine and that she needed help desperately but a person's pride was to be respected.

CHAPTER FOUR

"Actually there is something you can do for me," said Sita hesitantly.

"If I still had my rings, you would be welcome to them," said Lady Clara as she lifted up her hand and looked at her empty fingers.

"I wonder what happened to my rings."

"I don't want your rings, my lady," said Sita.

"Then what do you want?"

"A place to stay," said Sita quietly. "I and my maid, who is outside, we are looking for somewhere safe to stay awhile and if you offer us shelter my lady, then we will look after you a lot better than your servants have so far."

"Whom are you running from?" asked Lady Clara.

"My lady, it would be better if you don't know," said Sita urgently.

"So you are saying if I put you up here, you and your maid, Martha, is it?"

Sita nodded.

"Martha will look after me better than what my own servants are doing now?" She snorted.

"It cannot possibly get worse now, can it?"

"My lady, I don't know why your servants haven't dusted in here for ages, and have let the house go to rack and ruin, even the driveway is overgrown with grass."

"What?" croaked Lady Clara sitting up.

"Yes my lady. I don't know why your servants are giving you atrocious service but they are and I think it is time to let them go."

"Why would my servants serve me such an ill-turn?" asked Lady Clara plaintively.

Sita didn't know. She didn't care. As far as she was concerned it was criminal the way they have neglected their mistress and they have to pay for it.

"Who supervises your servants when you are ill and in bed?" Sita asked.

"I don't know," Lady Clara shook her head.

"Who pays them my lady?" prodded Sita.

"My man of affairs. Forgot his name, Ferret-face or something," she gave a vague wave of her hand.

Sita giggled.

Lady Clara looked at her strangely and said, "There is much merit in your idea, child. It warms my heart to hear your laughter. I believe you will do me much good."

"Do you really mean it?" asked Sita anxiously. It was the answer to her prayers.

"Never say anything I don't mean," said Lady Clara tartly.

Sita took a deep breath and closed her eyes. To be safe again, to not run anymore.

"I know what you shall do," cackled Lady Clara. "Tomorrow, you can come as my niece and bring that maid of yours. Demand to be shown to my room and take one look and sack the servants. I will agree with you."

Sita doubted if it would be that easy but she nodded anyway.

"Having doubts child?" asked Lady Clara shrewdly.

"I don't know about sacking of the servants, my lady," said Sita hesitantly.

"Nonsense! If you can't deal with a servant or two, you are not the resourceful young lady I think you are."

Sita paced worriedly.

"Now go away. I am feeling sleepy and come tomorrow morning."

And having given the order Lady Clara promptly fell asleep.

Sita came over to the bed and gazed down at the old lady looking so frail and wretched. She smoothed the hair from her brow and smiled.

"Good night, my lady," she said softly.

She slowly climbed out of the window and slid down the drainpipe until her feet found purchase in the ground.

Martha was there scolding her in whispers.

"What were you doing for so long milady? I thought you were caught. Who was there in the room?"

Sita held up a hand smiling and said, "Martha, I will tell you everything but come let's away from here."

"Yes milady, come, we should leave," said Martha and turned.

They made their long trek back to the rickety gate and to the gig that they left tucked under a tree away from sight.

They settled down in the gig and after they got comfortable Sita told Martha the conversation she had with Lady Clara Beddington.

"Milady, I don't know about this," sniffed Martha.

"Whatever is the matter with you, Martha?" asked Sita deciding to take the bull by its horns. "Aren't you happy with this plan? I promise you Lady Clara did invite us to stay at her home and to take the liberty of kicking her servants out, slovenly that they are."

"It might not be safe, milady. What if Squire

Grimes should come here?"

"Oh Martha, then it would be perfect," said Sita. "For he would not dare contradict Lady Clara and you should have heard her Martha, she was so haughty but she is nice."

Martha hunched a shoulder as she went about arranging their things. "It might be alright, I suppose."

"We will be safe again, Martha, think about that. You know how much we need that," said Sita pleadingly.

Martha looked her charge and sighed. It was true they needed a safe place and soon. They couldn't sleep on the gig forever, open to robbers and vagrants. She needed to get Lady Sita Andover to safety and this place, perhaps it would be the safe place they required.

"I can hear your thoughts, Martha," said Sita. "What are you thinking?"

"I am thinking that you be right, milady," said Martha. "It's about time you lived in a grand mansion again instead of a maid's cottage."

"Oh Martha, that isn't true, I enjoyed the cottage."

"Be it as it may be milady but for you to be in your proper surroundings is I am thinking a right blessing. Providing Lady Clara doesn't expect you to be maid to her," she looked suspiciously at Sita.

Sita laughed. "I doubt if Lady Clara has any

such intentions. For I am afraid I gave myself away," she confessed.

"How so milady?"

"Well, Lady Clara introduced herself so politely and held out her hand, like we were in her drawing room that I forgot myself and curtsied and kissed her hand. She knew immediately that I didn't learn that curtsy in any cottage."

"That be true milady."

"Although it is shameful the way she has been treated and by her own servants, mind you."

"You didn't tell her anything did you, milady?" asked Martha anxiously as a sudden doubt assailed her.

"No Martha," assured Sita. "I told her perfectly frankly that I cannot even give her my name and its better if she didn't know anything."

"And she agreed?"

"Yes, she said it cannot possibly get worse and then she said she believed I will do much good for her."

Martha sighed foreseeing a long interview with Lady Clara Beddington. But that will happen when it will, she thought philosophically.

"Good night milady, sleep well," said Martha as she tucked in Sita.

"Good night Martha," said Sita sleepily.

Martha took a long time falling asleep but

after she weighed all the pros and cons, she decided that they could do a lot worse and it wouldn't hurt to check the old lady out and see if Lady Sita could live in the grand mansion as befits the daughter of a Duke.

Especially after they kicked the servants out and finally milady can eat a roast chicken. God knows when the last time they ate a roast was, all they could afford was common pottage not that milady complained. She was such a dear and deserved so much better.

CHAPTER FIVE

"What if it all goes wrong Martha?" asked Sita the next morning seated in the back of the gig, hugging her basket nervously.

Martha flicked the reins and the horse trotted through the rickety gate and down the long drive and said soothingly, "It won't milady. Just be yourself, the daughter of a Duke and look all haughty and disapproving of everything around you. I will take care of the rest."

"We are in a gig, Martha," said Sita hysterically. "Oh lord, this is doomed to failure. What was I even thinking?"

"Hush milady," said Martha. "We will just tell them that one of the horses went lame and the chaise had to be left behind with the luggage. We borrowed the landlord's gig and here we are because you wanted to see your dear aunt."

Sita sighed and said, "Very well."

The gig turned the corner and rumbled to a

halt in front of the mansion. In daylight it was as imposing as it seemed at night but it also looked weary and tired. It had an unkempt look about it that made Sita angry as she thought of the poor lady lying in bed helpless and the shameless servants taking advantage of her.

Sita took a breath and exchanged glances with Martha and rang the doorbell loudly, clearly, and most insistently. In fact she didn't stop ringing until the door opened hastily and a butler stood there on the doorstep with a greasy food-stained waistcoat.

"Eh, what do you want making a noise like that?" he demanded angrily.

"I am here to see Lady Clara Beddington," she said crisply.

He glanced at her standing there spine ramrod straight with her maid by her side and asked uncertainly, "And who might you be?"

"It is none of your business," said Lady Sita haughtily "But I am Lady Clara's niece and I have come all the way from India to see my aunt. Step aside my good man and let us in."

"Lady Clara isn't receiving any visitors," said the butler bowing insultingly.

"I am not a visitor, I am her niece and if I don't gain entrance into the house immediately I will bring the magistrate upon you," said Sita angrily.

She stepped forward and ordered, "Step

aside."

The butler hastily stepped back before he was ploughed down by this determined young lady. He looked confused and angry.

"I am in need of refreshments, see to it."

"Don't keep her ladyship waiting, you idiot," said Martha as she pushed her way in elbowing the butler aside.

"Lady Clara made no mention of this," whined the butler.

"I cannot help that," said Lady Sita looking down her nose at him. "The arrangements were made a long time ago. No doubt it slipped her mind. She has not been well, I believe."

She gave him a penetrating glance, a look she perfected in the schoolroom as she was elder sister to eight young siblings. "I intend to see to her care myself."

"Stand aside nitwit," hissed Martha.

"Make room for your betters," she said saucily and flounced after her mistress who was making her way to the staircase.

"Stop!" shouted a large woman in a stained apron standing at the bottom of the stairs. "You can't go up there."

Sita sighed, "Martha, who is this creature?"

"I am the cook and housekeeper here," the woman said belligerently.

"I wouldn't shout that over the rooftops considering the lack of evidence we have here," said Sita disdainfully glancing around her as she picked up her skirts haughtily.

"Lady Clara cannot be disturbed."

"Says who?"

"She don't want to be seen."

"Nonsense! I am her niece and not her guest. Now, step aside woman"

"You can't....owww... you kicked me," she cried astonished at Martha who had kicked her hard on the ankle.

"Let's not waste time arguing with these people milady," advised Martha and together they both raced up the stairs.

They were followed in hot pursuit by the couple huffing and puffing.

Sita hurried to Lady Clara's bedchamber knocked perfunctorily and entered the room. The old lady was abed lying exactly as Sita had seen last night. She struggled to sit up and Sita rushed to help her.

"So you have come, niece. I wasn't sure if you would."

"Yes, I have come, my lady," said Sita as she moved to the curtains and drew them back to let the sun and some fresh breeze inside the room.

She turned and saw the other two servants had entered the room and she thought it prudent that she take the bull by its horns.

"Aunt, let me tell you, your servants have no manners for never have I been so insulted. They denied me entry into your house. Me?" said Sita proudly poised holding a hand upon her chest. "The daughter of a Duke that even the King would not dare deny entry."

"What's all this Weatherby?" demanded Lady Clara as she approved of Sita's stance and turned to spear the servants with her glittering eye.

"Milady, seeing that you are ill, we thought not to disturb you with any visitors," stammered the couple.

"Nonsense! She is my niece."

"And I absolutely refuse to let them remain here aunt. The house is filthy. Dismiss them this instance," demanded Sita haughtily.

"Well, you heard my niece," said Lady Clara irritably. "What are you waiting for? Get out."

"Are there any more servants in this house?" asked Martha suddenly.

"A footman and a maid," said the butler sullenly.

"Take them with you when you are going, will you?" said Sita sweetly and turned to Lady Clara.

"What about our wages?" demanded the cook.

"How dare you!" Sita turned on her in a rage. "I

have seen with my own eyes the appalling neglect of your mistress. You have taken advantage of her illness and you ought to be flogged. If papa were here, he would have had you flogged. I have no doubt you have cheated her out of money as well. Get out before I call the magistrate and have you arrested for common thieves that you are."

"Go on, git," said Martha pushing them out of the door. "Now mind no stealing the silver."

She winked at Sita and closed the door firmly behind them as she shepherded the couple of the room and out of the house.

CHAPTER SIX

"Well, that was entertaining," said Lady Clara with a laugh.

"Oh my lady, I trust we have done right," said Sita anxiously looking at her.

"We have my dear or rather you have," said Lady Clara approvingly. "Although I cannot imagine how I ever tolerated these people, perhaps they came to me after I became ill."

"Well, my lady, the first thing we have to do is give you a nice bath," said Sita determinedly. "You would like that, wouldn't you? And a cleaning of this room and perhaps, a soft-boiled egg with toast."

"A soft boiled egg?" the old lady repeated in a whisper. "I haven't had that since…" she broke off her voice choking.

"I will get Martha, my lady and we will see about getting you right comfortable again," said Sita hurriedly as she stepped out of the room.

She ran into Martha in the Great Hall as she stood watching the butler and the cook leave the premises with the maid and footman sullenly following them.

"I see what you meant milady," said Martha quietly. "The poor lady. It is wicked the condition she is in."

"Yes Martha but what are we to do now?" asked Sita worried nibbling at her lower lip. "I promised Lady Clara she would have a bath and a clean room and a nice soft boiled egg."

"Well, let me get to work milady but first let's see what is there in the kitchen."

And so they trooped down to the kitchen only to find it empty of people. Martha sighed and set the kettle to boil for some hot water. Just as they were discussing how to carry hot water to the second floor when in walked the farmer's boy with fresh eggs and milk.

Martha instantly pounced upon him and set him to work and she pushed Sita out of the kitchen and said, "Milady, why don't you go and look at the other rooms and decide on one reasonably clean, so we can shift Lady Clara there, for cleaning her current room will take ages."

"Okay Martha," said Sita obediently and went room hunting.

Soon she found a beautiful room done in warm yellow tones that looked all sunny and bright and cheerful. Once she whipped the Holland covers away it was just perfect only a little dusting was required which she gladly got to and by the time she finished she heard Martha calling to her.

She stepped out of the room onto the landing and said, "I am here Martha. I found the perfect room for Lady Clara."

Martha approved of the room and soon went carrying jugs of hot water to Lady Clara's bedchamber and pressed the farmer's boy into carrying the bath tub. He also gently lowered the old lady into the tub were Martha gave her good wash. Sita washed the old lady's hair.

"You must cut it, my lady," she said sadly looking at the mess the hair was in.

"Well, do so if you have a mind to," said Lady Clara.

Martha got out the scissors and soon tamed the dirty hair and after a rinse it lay soft and fresh across the old lady's shoulders.

Lady Clara sighed loudly, "I feel wonderful."

"You will feel even better in your new bedchamber, my lady," said Sita confidently.

She instructed the farmer's boy to carry Lady Clara to the first floor where the Yellow Room was located.

Lady Clara was delighted with her new room and she said so with a smile.

Martha walked in with her soft-boiled egg and toast and weak tea and soon she was tucking into the breakfast like she hadn't eaten in years.

After breakfast she just lay there and said, "I am tired now and I would like to sleep but you must pick a room for yourself and your maid and be comfortable now. I would like to see you when I awake."

"I will, my lady," said Sita as she curtsied and went out of the room.

She went in search of Martha whom she found busy in the kitchen talking to the farmer's boy.

"Milady, is there anything you want?" asked Martha as soon as she saw Sita step into the kitchen.

"We need an army of servants to put this place in order, Martha," said Sita sitting down at the ancient wooden table and leaning her chin onto the palm of her hand.

"Don't you worry milady, I have just been asking Bill here," she pointed to the farmer's boy.

"And he said all the original servants of the house live at the village now and they would be right glad to get their jobs back."

"The original servants?"

"Yes milady, apparently the agent of Lady Clara…"

"Ferret-face," said Sita absently.

"Yes, milady, he dismissed them all and installed these two in their stead when milady fell ill."

"We have to see to ferret-face as well Martha"

"Don't worry milady one thing at a time," said Martha consolingly.

"Bill, why don't you go on up to the village and inform the old servants to come back. And go to your mother and ask for some fresh butter and more milk and eggs."

Bill nodded and gave a cheery wave as he sped off on his errand.

"Now, how about some breakfast and some hot tea? You haven't had a thing to eat since morning."

"That would be lovely," exclaimed Sita as she stood up to prepare herself some tea.

"Oh no, you don't, milady," admonished Martha. "You just sit there and let us get you your breakfast like it should be."

"Martha, I don't mind," said Sita softly.

"Well, I do," snapped Martha. "Its high time you were treated like a lady and here we will start right. From tomorrow as soon as the servants clean the place, you will have your breakfast in the breakfast parlour and your dinner in the dining room."

Sita laughed and said, "I thought you would banish me to the nursery."

"I might well do so, milady," twinkled Martha as she bustled about the kitchen.

After breakfast and conferring with Martha the immediate work that would needs be done, and overseeing the servants who started pouring in once word was out that Sita stepped up to check on Lady Clara with a luncheon tray.

She found the lady crying.

"My lady, what happened?" asked Sita concerned as she placed the tray on the bedside table.

Lady Clara held on to her hands and squeezed them tightly as fresh tears ran down her face.

"You are a dear child," she said.

"I am glad you like your new room," said Sita. "Why don't you have some lunch while I tell you what Martha and I have been up to?"

So while Lady Clara slowly began eating healthy food once again, Sita filled her in on the condition of the house and the fact that all her old servants were still at the village and would gladly come back to work.

Lady Clara nodded pleased to hear that and as the long afternoon fell, they could hear muffled noises coming from everywhere inside and outside the house.

Sita stepped up to the window and glanced out to see an army of servants cutting the overgrown grass in the driveway.

Two weeks passed peacefully.

CHAPTER SEVEN

Sita had just left Lady Clara's room and was coming down the stairs when she heard the front doorbell ringing in the hall below.

A visitor? Whoever could it be?

She heard Claude, the butler answer the door and a deep voice said, "I am here to see Lady Clara Beddington. Inform her that the Earl of Stonebridge is here to pay his respects."

Sita peered over the balcony railing but all could see what a tall figure with a caped coat and a hat imposing enough as it is but with a walking stick in his hand.

Claude bowed and said, "If you would step this way, milord, I will inform her ladyship of your arrival."

He then proceeded to show the guest into the morning room. Sita ran down the steps just as Claude stepped into the hall once again and shut the door.

"Claude, perhaps you can inform Lady Clara of

her visitor, I will see to the tea."

"Yes milady," said Claude pained at the liberty Sita was wont to take between upstairs and downstairs.

Sita ran down to the kitchen and grabbed Martha, "The Earl of Stonebridge is here to see Lady Clara."

"Well, what of it?" asked Martha confused.

"What will Lady Clara tell of us?"

"Don't worry milady, perhaps Lady Clara will just send him on his way."

Unfortunately that wasn't true for the summons arrived soon thereafter, a politely worded request for Lady Sita to step into the morning room.

Sita with trepidation walked into the morning room and there standing with his back to the fireplace was the most magnificent specimen of a man she had ever seen.

He was imposingly tall, wearing a blue superfine coat with silver buttons, a white ruffled shirt and black breeches and high black boots that shined so much it hurt her eye just to look at them.

Despite the height of his fashionable attire, he wasn't the pale pink like his fellows but beautifully tanned that threw his aristocratic features into high relief.

"Come in my dear," invited Lady Clara seated as she was on the sofa with a Cashmere shawl wrapped around her. "Meet my nephew, Julian

Stonebridge, just returned from India. And Julian this here is my guardian angel, Lady Sita."

Sita instinctively dropped into a curtsy but at the revelation of her name, she gasped and looked at horror at Lady Clara.

Lady Clara winked at her and turned to her nephew. "What wild horses dragged you from the fabled East, Julian?"

Julian gave an exquisite bow but noted the look of horror that passed over the beautiful face and the wink that his aunt gave her. Some mischief was no doubt afoot which he probably ought to nip in the bud but he pushed it aside and said brusquely, "You brought me here aunt."

"Me?" asked Lady Clara astonished.

"When none of my letters were answered and it has been nearly a year since I received so much as a note from you, I was worried and so thought to bring myself over to see how you were doing."

"But I didn't receive any of your letters," protested Lady Clara. "I thought you all but forgot about me."

"Forgotten about you?" asked a shocked Julian. "How is that even possible? And why didn't you receive any of my letters?" he asked suspiciously darting a glance at the beauty sitting beside his aunt like a prim statue.

"Now don't stare at Lady Sita my love, she only came here a fortnight ago. It must be those useless servants of mine, whom ferret-face hired and who saw fit to slowly kill me."

"Servants? Ferret-face? Kill you?"

"Oh it's a long story but the long and short of it is that the agent you appointed threw my old servants out and brought in some new ones. I didn't even know of the change since I was grievously ill."

"Aunt Clara, how are you now dear?" he spoke quietly with a great deal of affection in his voice.

Sita felt a lump in her throat. To have someone care of her, she sighed, it wasn't meant to be.

"I am fine, Julian, dear Sita has been taking such wonderful good care of me"

"Pardon me aunt but who is she?"

"Why, she is my niece and your cousin," lied Lady Clara outrageously.

Julian's lips quivered for a moment and he squashed the smile and said, "My cousin, you say?"

"Of course dear boy, daresay you won't remember all your cousins," said Lady Clara with a vaguely dismissive gesture.

"Since I am an only child and so are you, I fail to see how I have earned a cousin miraculously but I will let it be for now," said Julian dismissively.

"No doubt you are tired after such a long journey," nodded Lady Clara. "Ring the bell dear, a little rest will do you a world of good. Ah, Claude, please show Lord Stonebridge to his chambers and see to it that he is comfortable. We will meet for dinner."

Having thus summarily dismissed her guest who made a bow and took himself off to his chambers to rest, Lady Clara turned to Sita and said, "There child, no need to worry. Martha gave me your name and a little bit of who you are. Your secret is safe with me dear and it's a good thing Julian is here as well because he will take care of things, you will see."

"My lady, I am sorry for the deception," apologised Sita.

"I thought we decided that I am an aunt to you."

"Aunt Clara, thank you."

"Thank you, child. If it wasn't for you I would in all probability be dead by now."

Sita made a distressed sound with tears clouding her eyes.

"There child I am not dead yet. Call Claude and tell him I would like to go to my room and will probably take lunch there. I feel a need to rest some."

Sita called Claude and fussed over the old lady as she was carried to her room.

She spent the afternoon restlessly unsure of what to do and how to proceed.

Martha was of no help, she merely smiled and said it will work out and spent the afternoon going through the gowns Lady Clara had given Lady Sita to decide which will have to be reworked for an evening gown.

"So that's Lady Clara's nephew?" said Martha selecting a gown that she set about working on.

"I imagined him quite different," said Sita sitting on the chair by the window.

"Different, how?"

"Well, not someone so top-lofty I suppose," said Sita. "Oh Martha did you see his clothes? They were perfection itself."

"Hmm."

"And it's disgraceful how he stayed away for years."

"Hmm."

"He is very handsome, isn't he?" Sita sighed.

Martha snorted "Handsome is as handsome does miss, don't you go forgetting that."

But secretly Martha thought it would be ideal if romance was in the air for Sita was tall and slender with penny gold hair, sky blue eyes and an exquisite beauty that gave the world an impression of the delicacy of gilded crystal.

Dinner was fraught with tension for Lady Sita sat awaiting denouement any moment and dreading it. But Aunt Clara and Julian chatted away comfortably. Taking turns filling each other in with all the family information until talk turned towards India.

Sita jerked startled and blushed rosily when

others turned to look at her.

"You know my lady," said Julian conversationally looking at Sita. "That's a very unusual name you have there."

Sita nodded "I believe so my lord."

"In fact if memory serves me correct, it is the name of one of the Hindu goddesses in India."

"Goddesses Julian?" asked Aunt Clara.

"Of course aunt, a Hindu deity I believe."

Aunt Clara shot Sita a look and then deftly turned the conversation into other mundane topics.

"Have you brought your horses with you, Julian?" she demanded.

"They should be here tonight, Aunt Clara," smiled Julian.

"Poor Sita here hasn't even a hack that she can ride except for that sway-backed monster she calls a horse."

"What happened to your own horses Aunt?"

"I really don't remember Julian, perhaps I sold them."

"Perhaps it was stolen," said Sita softly.

"Yes that agent of mine is no good. See to it that he is dismissed Julian," commanded Aunt Clara.

"With pleasure Aunt," he said.

"Well dinner was excellent but I am plump tired, Claude take me to my room please and send my maid to me."

Sita stood up hurriedly. "I will help Aunt Clara."

"Nonsense child. Stay and entertain Julian. It must seem an odd homecoming for him if we were all to disappear to our beds."

Sita hovered by the door in indecision and then finally bowed to the inevitable and stepped back into the room and said, "Would you like some tea, my lord?"

Julian nodded and said "Tea sounds delightful my lady, perhaps in the adjoining saloon?"

She nodded and quickly walked out of the dining room and watched the slow progress made by Claude and Lady Clara up the stairs and then feeling the presence of Lord Stonebridge behind her she quickly walked into the adjoining saloon and rang for some tea.

She sat on the sofa and gracefully gestured to a chair and said, "Please be seated my lord, tea will be brought in shortly."

Julian sat on the chair opposite hers, "So my lady, how come you to bear an unusual Hindu name?" he asked.

Sita looked startled for a moment and then said resignedly, "It was my mama's choice my lord, having lived in India before."

"Really?" asked Julian astonished. "Who is your mother? Perhaps I might have met her."

"Mama is no more my lord," said Sita sadly.

"I am sorry to hear that my lady," said Julian softly.

"A loss we must bear having felt it too keenly," said Sita.

The tea service was wheeled in and she began to disperse the tea and biscuits.

"Tell me my lord, how do you like India?" she asked curiously.

"It's a fabulous place once you get used to the heat," said Julian.

"Is it as colourful as it is said?"

"Far more than mere words can describe my lady. It's like an explosion of colour."

"Do you miss it?"

"Perhaps, it's early yet to say with any certainty but one day I would like to visit again."

"Did you travel on elephants, my lord?" asked Sita excitedly.

Julian looked surprised and said "You seem to be well-acquainted with the modes of travel there, my lady.

Sita vaguely gestured and said, "On account of my mother my lord."

"Ah yes, your mother," said Julian strangely.

Sita stood up uncomfortable and made a graceful curtsy, "I will leave you to enjoy your drink my lord; for I too would like to retire."

Julian stood up and bowed, "Good night milady."

CHAPTER EIGHT

Sita woke early the next morning for she hardly slept the night before. One tall imposing man clouded her thoughts. She got out of the bed and walked to the window and breathed in the fresh morning air and then she heard it. The neighing. The horses. They have arrived.

She turned to dash down to the stables when Martha walked in with her breakfast.

"Now, where are you off to missy?" she asked crossly.

"Oh Martha," breathed Sita "The horses."

"They will be there even after you have had your breakfast and your bath and changed your bedclothes to something more presentable for company."

Sita blushed looking at her white silk nightgown and sat down in the chair by the window.

She waited patiently for Martha to pour her a cup of hot tea and place the sandwiches in front of her.

"Martha, Aunt Clara said I could go riding," she said excitedly.

"Is that so milady?"

"It has been so long since I had ridden a horse Martha. Oh you know what I mean, a thoroughbred like papa used to have. Remember how mama and papa used to ride out every day and people used to actually come out of their houses to stare at them as they passed by."

"Your mother was a beautiful lady," said Martha reminiscing.

"True. Think you can find me a riding habit, Martha. I want to ride astride like mama used to."

"But milady," protested Martha shocked.

"Martha, I don't know any other manner of riding," overrode Sita. "Be a dear and find me a habit."

Martha sniffed and went out of the room.

Sita sat and watched the gardeners come and begin their daily work of clearing the grounds. At least the driveway was mowed of all grass thought Sita proudly.

Then she saw Lord Stonebridge walk from the house to the stables putting on his riding gloves. Sita leaned forward as she watched him enter the stables and then shortly thereafter exit the stables riding an Arabian. She almost swooned in envy.

She waited impatiently for Martha to find her a habit. When Martha finally brought her one, it was a beautiful bottle green riding habit that probably belonged to Lady Clara.

"Now milady this seems to be the only one that will fit and it is cut for the side saddle."

"Oh what use is it to me then, Martha?" wailed Sita. "It's beautiful no doubt but I can hardly wear it. I wouldn't know how to ride side saddle."

"Perhaps milady if you were to wear your muslin," suggested Martha.

"I can?" asked Sita round-eyed.

"I don't see why not milady" said Martha pursuing her lips thoughtfully. "The Earl would return shortly from his ride and hole himself up in his study. Lady Clara will be in her chambers and there won't be anyone to see you ride, milady."

"Oh Martha, that is brilliant," said Sita hugging Martha enthusiastically.

She had her bath and got dressed quickly and went to look in on Lady Clara who looked at her approvingly and said, "Don't you look like a picture, Sita"

Sita blushed and said, "Aunt Clara if there is anything you require?"

"No, my dear, I am fine. I will ring for my maid if I do require anything"

"I just thought to step out to the stables Aunt Clara and look at the horses."

"Please do child and if any horse catches your fancy, feel free to take it for a ride; although you be careful, Julian's horses are thoroughbreds and not easy-steppers."

Sita laughed and said, "I will be careful Aunt Clara."

She ran down the stairs and waved cheerfully at Claude and went to the stables. Soon she lost all sense of time as she was petting and crooning to the most magnificent beasts she has ever seen, each better than the other.

The stable master looked upon knowingly and said, "Would you like to select a horse to ride, milady?"

"I would love to," said Sita. "Perhaps the Black?"

"Be careful milady," warned the stable master. "That one has got a temper."

"What? This pretty little boy," crooned Sita as the Black nuzzled at her hair. She walked it towards a mounting block and soon sat astride.

Then with a cheery wave to the stable master she slowly trotted the horse out of the stables through the long driveway and out on to the grounds of the estate.

She wheeled the horse and spurred it into a gallop making for the copse of beech trees in the distance. She laughed at her freedom and rode recklessly jumping over hedges and fallen down tree trunks.

She finally pulled to a stop near a silent pond

and slid down her horse's back and rubbed him down and led him to the water.

She sat on the bank and watched her horse drink the water thirstily when a hand grabbed her shoulder and a voice shouted, "Got you!"

She screamed and turned, "Squire Grimes?"

"Thought to escape me eh?" said the Squire advancing towards her. "I searched all over for you, Mrs Mallory and what do I find, you sitting in that big mansion pretending to be some old lady's niece."

"Stay right where you are, sir," commanded Sita her hand going to her dagger tucked in her ribbon around the waist.

"Oh like that puny thing is going to stop me," said the Squire rubbing his hands.

Before she could free the dagger from the ribbon, he grabbed her. Her terrified scream was muffled by his soft pudgy hand. She immediately began fighting blindly thrashing against his iron grip.

"Shut up" he growled and dragged her by her hair away from the pond.

She was flung aside like as if she was a rag doll. She looked up in wide-eyed terror.

"Entering a mansion under false pretences eh my gel? And sacking the servants," he shook his head. "Not very well done of you. Why, they were eager enough to tell me tales about you and where to find you."

A sickening knowing spiralled down to the pit of her stomach paralyzing her. Struggling for calm, Sita swallowed hard gripping the dagger harder. He squeezed her breast. She sobbed.

"Don't do this," she pleaded.

"Told you everything's going to be fine, long as you spread your legs for me."

"No," she screamed as he lowered his stinking mouth and tried to kiss her. She bit his lips and he slapped her.

She screamed again while he clamped his meaty hand over her mouth. She fought against his brute strength. He flung himself atop of her and ground himself on her.

"Nice and easy," he said leering at her as he tore at her bodice.

She got her dagger free and plunged it in his arm.

"You bitch," he shouted and slapped her hard. She screamed fighting against him madly.

The details of the next few minutes she could never recall clearly afterwards.

She only knew that she kept plunging her knife into his arm and suddenly his weight was lifted off of her.

"You bastard," shouted the Earl of Stonebridge. And he pummelled him.

"Hey, she is mine," squealed the Squire.

"Over my dead body" said the Earl as he lifted his arm and belted him one right across the jaw that dropped the Squire down to the ground.

"Ahh, my sweet," said the Earl as he rushed to her and helped her sit up.

"He…he…" she muttered looking dazed.

"I know sweetling, I know," he said gently removing the dagger from her hand.

Sita looked at it strangely as if it was a thing removed from her body. She noticed her fingers were bloodied and vaguely wondered why and then she looked up at the Earl.

"He wanted to be my protector and so we ran away and Aunt Clara…."

"You are safe now sweetheart," said the Earl concerned as he wrapped his coat around her tattered dress.

"Come, let's get you back home."

"No, it's not safe," she shrank back.

"I have to go…" she looked about her wildly.

"It is safe, sweetling, I promise you," crooned the Earl holding her by the waist close to him.

"Sshhh….just breathe sweetheart. Everything will be alright, I promise you. No one will ever harm you again. Come Martha and Aunt Clara are worried about you."

She let herself be coaxed and lifted onto his

stallion and he climbed behind her and took the reins. He rode hell for leather to the mansion.

She hid her face in the folds of his shirt and smelled the sandalwood and oddly it was deeply comforting for her. She clutched his shirt but the tears wouldn't stop coursing through her cheeks.

He held her tightly against him aware of her fragility and delicate state. He prayed Martha and Aunt Clara knew what to say to her.

He arrived at the Stonebridge mansion which had servants swarming all over the place.

He stopped at the front and got down and gently lifted Sita off the horse's back and carried her into the house.

Claude dropped his placid demeanour and looked on in shock at the Earl carrying milady up the stairs. "Milord!"

"Get Martha, Claude, hurry," said the Earl as he carried Sita up to her chambers.

CHAPTER NINE

Martha burst into the chambers like a little whirlwind just as the Earl was placing Sita on top of the bed.

"What is this? What happened?" she cried.

"She was attacked in the meadow, Martha," replied the Earl.

"Oh my god! Who would do this?" cried Martha as she hurriedly checked out Sita.

"Martha," cried Sita.

"Hush, dear, I am here," crooned Martha as she got a bowl of water and started cleaning her up.

"It was Squire Grimes, Martha," whispered Sita. "He wanted....he wanted…"

"There now. He is not going to get whatever he wanted. Don't you worry milady," said Martha angrily.

"Who is Squire Grimes?" asked the Earl.

"He desires Lady Sita and when she rejected his advances, he made some very inappropriate comments which prompted us to leave and ...." stopped Martha abruptly.

"And come here" finished Julian suavely.

"Begging your pardon milord but I will have to clean milady up," said Martha.

"Of course, and please inform her that Squire or not, she is safe from all harm here. No one will take her from Stonebridge without her consent," vowed Julian and left the room.

Aunt Clara was beside herself with worry when Julian stopped by and informed her of what happened.

"How did you find her Julian?"

"Pure chance madam" said Julian pacing his aunt's bedchamber. "I was returning from my ride and heard a scream and so I turned towards the copse of beechwood trees and there I found Lady Sita tussling with a man. She had a dagger with her and although she tried she was only able to hurt his arm."

The door opened and in stepped Claude.

"You rang milord?"

"Yes Claude," said Julian coldly. "Send out a few able-bodied fellows to the meadow where the beechwood trees are and there by the pond you will find a man lying hurt and unconscious. Tie him and drag him here. And also, bring milady's horse."

"Yes, milord," said Claude and promptly turned to order the footmen.

"According to Martha, this Squire Grimes fellow was persecuting Lady Sita already and that's what prompted them to leave the place they were in and come here, Aunt Clara."

He turned and speared his aunt with a glance "And what do you know about that?"

"I was told that the place where they stayed earlier was sullied by the presence of this obnoxious fellow and so they were forced to leave there and by happy chance come here."

"What is it you are not telling me aunt?" asked Julian.

"It's not my story to tell dear Julian" said Aunt Clara simply.

He sighed and ran his fingers through his hair. "I need a drink"

"Well go on downstairs, I will have Martha come to you and update you on Lady Sita's condition."

"Thank you aunt," said Julian stiffly and took himself off to the study where the poured a drink and stared out of the window. He should have bloody killed the fellow right there he thought.

A discrete knock sounded on the door and in stepped Claude.

"Milord, the person was not in the place you mentioned," he said clearly. "Milady's horse on the other hand has been brought back to the stables safe and sound."

"What?" stared Julian blankly.

"The said person whom the footmen were supposed to drag in here tied was not be found."

"But I left him there and he was unconscious at that time," muttered Julian.

"Perhaps he regained consciousness and thought it prudent to escape milord?" suggested Claude.

"Dammit!" shouted Julian. "I want his head on a platter. Send men out Claude and have him traced for me. His name is Squire Grimes and I want every nasty bit of detail on him."

"At once milord," said Claude and respectfully withdrew.

Irritated Julian downed another drink and contemplated going upstairs to see for himself if Sita was alright when there was a brisk knock on the door and it opened and in stepped Martha.

"Lady Clara requested I update you milord on milady's condition," she said and gave a little bob of curtsy.

"How is she, Martha?"

"In shock milord but physically no harm has occurred."

"Thank the lord I arrived just in time," said Julian.

"I thank you milord for your timely rescue of milady," began Martha when Julian held up his hand to stop the flow of words.

"What's with this obsession Martha?"

"I don't know milord," said Martha helplessly. "The couple of times he attempted to court milady, she laughed at him and then one day he just turned up at our doorstep offering himself as her protector and promised he would come to her that night and so we had no choice but to pack our belongings and leave the place. We came here and milady found Lady Clara in a sickened condition with the servants mistreating her and everything going to rack and ruin. She decided that she would help Lady Clara get well and Lady Clara decided she might just as well be her niece while she is at it. That's how you came upon us milord."

Julian allowed the silence to fill the study as he observed Martha fidget restlessly under his steady gaze.

"There is more to this than meets the eye Martha."

"Yes milord."

"And yet, this is all I am to be accorded with."

"Yes milord."

"What is it that you aren't telling me?"

"It isn't my tale to tell milord," said Martha frightened. "Please milord don't ask milady not after what she has gone through."

"How is she doing now?"

"She is in bed milord, falling asleep as I came downstairs."

"Alright, you may leave now."
Martha curtsied and left the study.

CHAPTER TEN

It was late afternoon when Julian climbed the stairs to go his chambers. Martha was downstairs with the servants having her lunch and Aunt Clara had hers on a tray in her room. On a sudden impulse he decided to look in on Lady Sita.

He gently pulled her door open and peered in not wanting to intrude on her privacy when he heard some distressed whimpering. He stepped fully into the room when he saw Sita sit up on the bed and climb out of it and walk to a corner of the room. She hadn't noticed him for he was at the far end of the room.

She sank onto the floor in the corner and then struck a match with which she lit an oil lamp placed nearby. In the flare of the light he could make out a painting of a man and a woman smiling at the world and another painting of a blue man playing a flute - Krishna!

He remembered from his days in India that he was a revered god for the Hindus. He silently observed Sita fold her hands together palms facing each other as she closed her eyes and gently breathed in and out. He felt a strange peace drifting towards him. He watched for a while and then silently stepped out of the room.

He walked on to his rooms and closed the door behind him. There was too much food for thought. And none of which he could make head or tail of but one thing was very clear, there was a mystery to Lady Sita which apparently had both her maid and his aunt feeling very protective towards her.

He went to the anteroom where his luggage was stored and after searching amongst the boxes there he finally found what he was looking for, a porcelain figurine. He looked at it as he absently traced the figure and after coming to a decision, he took it with him downstairs.

Dinner was a solitary affair since Lady Sita refused to come down and Aunt Clara preferred to dine in her chamber. Frustrated Julian ate alone.

The news that Claude brought him along with his dinner that Squire Grimes vacated his room at the local village inn and was nowhere to be found contributed to his anger. He instructed his men to chase the Squire down to whichever county he was in and bring him word as soon as they found him.

He finished his dinner and went to his study afterwards for a drink. It lay in the end of the wing housing Sita's bedchamber, one floor down. The windows were long reaching from floor to ceiling.

The curtains tied back, the windows overlooked shrubbery and a section of wilderness that the gardeners had yet to get to. He could make out the brown canopies of the woodland beyond. It was pleasant in the afternoon with the smell of mown grass and lush meadows in the distant.

He heard a soft click as the door to the study was opened and soft footsteps entering. He turned frowning at the intrusion when his frown turned to surprise on perceiving it was Lady Sita clutching at the door behind her as she closed it.

"My lady?" questioned Julian not moving from his stance by the window for fear he would send her running back to her room.

"I wanted to thank you my lord for rescuing me," she said softly.

"I am sorry you had to go through such an ordeal my lady on my lands. I can only apologise for the pain all this has caused you," said Julian concerned.

"Martha said the Squire must be deranged to follow me so and force his attentions on me"

Julian held his peace for frankly he could hardly fault the Squire by being besotted by this radiant beauty standing in front of him.

"How are you feeling now, my lady?" he inquired solicitously.

"Much better my lord," said Sita restlessly as she wandered further into the room. "Martha informed me that you sent out people to trace the whereabouts of Squire Grimes."

"That is correct my lady," nodded Julian. "I will see he is brought to justice."

"Oh I thank you for that my lord but wouldn't it be better if we were to ignore what happened?" asked Sita anxiously coming to stand in front of him.

Looking at big sea-blue eyes deep in worry made his heart clench but Julian said, "It would only encourage him to prey on others my lady."

"But I don't want to testify," said Sita tears springing to her eyes.

"Ah my sweetling," said Julian setting aside his drink and taking her into his arms. "There will be no need for you to testify. I will arrange matters in such a way as to punish him and yet leave you completely out of the picture. You are safe, my love."

Sita stared up at him in wonder. Julian dipped his head a fraction and gently kissed her lips. She felt the slow heat wash through her, a tide of simple delight that left her tingling all over.

He drew back and walked towards his desk. Sita turned and watched him under her hooded eyes nibbling her lips worriedly.

"I thought to give you a gift," said Julian as he rummaged through his desk and brought out a porcelain figure.

"I shouldn't accept," protested Sita.

"Please do," said Julian handing over the figurine. "I think you will appreciate this more than I."

Sita gingerly took the figurine in her hands and turned it facing front forwards and gasped aloud.

"Krishna!"

"I knew you would like this gift," said a satisfied Julian.

"But how did you...?" asked Sita confused clutching the figurine to her bosom.

Julian watched her bosom heave and mentally sighed and said, "With a name like yours, it seemed natural."

Sita blushed. "I thank you, my lord. I will treasure it always."

"Julian," he said.

"I beg your pardon."

"My name is Julian and perhaps you should start calling me by that."

"My lord, I don't think..."

"Sshhh..." said Julian laying a finger on her lips. "Don't think just feel."

He moved closer and slowly traced her lips with his fingers holding her gaze all the time and watched her eyes widen with shock and darken with desire as he slipped a finger into her mouth and bring it out.

He deftly removed the figurine from her lifeless fingers and placed it on the table. He replaced his finger with his tongue spanning her waist with his hands and bringing her closer.

She lifted her arms and placed it on his shoulders dragging him closer to her. She opened her mouth to him on a soft moan and revelled in his response. She became softer as he became harder.

And with his hardness came the heat. It rose like a fever turning the swirling pleasure hot. His fingers slowly traced her body curves and slid over her breasts making her gasp.

He lifted his head to look at her questioningly. She clung closer to him in response hiding her face in his shoulder as her breast pressed into the palm of his hand.

His fingers firmed possessively cupping her soft flesh now swollen with need she didn't understand. Her nipples ached for his touch and when he stroked them she actually moaned loudly.

With every ounce of his experience Julian deliberately drew her deeper into a whirlpool of desire. She was naïve, innocent and she needed to be coaxed to passion gently, loved tenderly and he was just the man to do it.

She was willing even eager and the knowledge stirred his passions powerfully. Her innocence was refreshing, heady, addictive and utterly entrancing. He deliberately lifted his head from kissing her and waited stroking her breast, Sita's eyes widened under heavy lids as she watched him pull down the sleeves of her bodice.

Her breasts sprung free under his watchful gaze. She was aghast, and utterly smitten. Her every nerve calling for his hand to palm her breast.

Julian watched her reaction, watched passion flare in those beautiful sea-blue eyes as he gently kneaded her breast. He bent his head and she lifted her face for his kiss when he dipped his head lower and placed a kiss on her throat. She gasped. He nibbled, he licked, he bit and Sita clung to him like an anchor in her suddenly swirling world of desire.

The heat of his mouth, the sweep of his tongue scalded her and she gave a strangled cry. Julian stilled his ministrations; he didn't want to lose her. He wanted her for a lifetime.

With his hands, mouth, lips and tongue, he gently soothed her fevered flesh, took the sting from her aches, the edge from her passion and eased her gently into pleasure.

She slowly came to her senses, flowing with the tide her mind steady. When full consciousness came there was no shock. She wanted this. The continuing touch of Julian's hands, the caress of his lips, his tongue was all familiar, safe and no threat.

Carefully he drew back and smiled at the soft glow that lit up her face removing all trace of fear and concern that was there previously.

He pulled her bodice up and tucked her hair

behind her ear and dropped a kiss atop her golden hair flowing in the wind.

"Ah sweetling, you are too much temptation for one ordinary man," he sighed.

Sita blushed as she hurriedly righted her clothes.

Julian watched her closely and then said, "You don't have any regrets do you?" he asked.

She turned in surprise and shook her head. "I would probably regret if it didn't happen, my lord," she said softly.

Julian was entranced. "Well, then we must see to it that we have cause enough to make it happen often."

Sita blushed and dropped her head.

"Sita, there is no easy way to do this but I shall ask this blandly, will you marry me sweetling? I know there are secrets you hold close to your chest and I will not pry into them. Time will tell if I am worthy enough of your confidences but this I know for a fact that I cannot imagine my life without you and I promise I will guard you with my life," Julian said and shrugged his shoulders.

Sita stood shocked.

"If I knew where your parents were I would ask them permission to court you and marry you but I don't and you are here and so am I. I can keep you safe from whatever it is that is bothering you and you don't ever have to worry about anything ever again."

Sita stood silent and sadly remembered her parents and what Martha said when they were coming to Stonebridge mansion. Perhaps it is the right decision to marry Julian. He was all that was good and kind.

She wondered about Dominic and her sisters and brothers but she also knew that she wanted a lifetime with this gentle and kind man who showed her so much of compassion and love.

She nodded hesitantly and said softly, "Yes, I will marry you, Julian."

CHAPTER ELEVEN

Aunt Clara was absolutely delighted with the turn of events when she was apprised of the facts the next morning.

"It's about time you set up your own nursery, Julian," she said approvingly. "Instead of gallivanting around the world."

Julian nodded and smiled at her enthusiasm.

Martha was beside herself with joy.

"Oh you made the right decision milady," she assured her.

"But Martha, what about Dominic?" asked Sita worriedly. "What about my brothers and sisters? I don't even know where they are and how they are."

"Well, the good Lord in heaven will take care of them milady just like he took care of you. You must have faith. The Earl is a good man for all his jaunting around the world but I suppose once you are married, he will be happy to stay here and see to his family."

"Oh Martha," sighed Sita. "To have a family once again and to be safe and not to run and worry ever again."

"No less than you deserve after all that you have been through," said Martha grimly.

Aunt Clara when Sita approached her with trepidation told her flatly and to her face that Julian could not have done better.

"I would much rather see you as mistress to Stonebridge than any one of those simpering London misses, I will tell you that Sita," she said tartly and banished any lingering doubts that Sita might have had and so happily she immersed herself in the preparations for her upcoming wedding.

It was decided that they will wed quietly at the Stonebridge chapel with the local vicar officiating the ceremony. Sita was pleased she would remain here at Stonebridge and not have to travel to London.

Aunt Clara declared that they were to have an engagement ball if only to announce the upcoming wedding to the local gentry.

"For mind you, Julian, I am not having the wedding done in a havey-cavey manner like it was a dashed hole-in-the-wall affair."

Julian and Sita both agreed to the engagement ball primarily to keep Aunt Clara happy.

Julian was pleased that he could show Sita off to his people and Sita was worried that she would be dancing at parties when she promised she would remain in hiding.

Martha when applied to said wisely, "It's only a local affair milady. People hereabouts are already familiar with your presence in the Stonebridge mansion. And with the announcement of the engagement, it will give an air of respectability to your presence here."

"But Martha, Aunt Clara was here the entire time as chaperon," protested Sita.

"That be true milady but tongues wag notwithstanding and the Earl is a prime catch here and so it's only right and proper that we send out the message loud and clear that he is taken."

Sita laughed till her sides hurt, "Oh Martha, you are so absurd."

Martha smiled indulgently at her charge rolling on the bed and said, "Come milady, let's go through the fabric from the attic that Lady Clara has generously given us and see if any colour you like that we can give to the village seamstress to stich for the wedding and the engagement ball."

Sita sat up her ears perking at that, "Yes Martha, let's do that. This is so exciting."

"Now why don't you take a turn about the gardens while I instruct the footmen to bring down the chests?" suggested Martha.

"Splendid idea. I will walk in the gardens," said Sita as she stepped out of the room and made her way down the stairs.

She passed the study and heard voices coming from there and thought Julian must have visitors and so she turned about and went through the kitchens into the gardens.

She looked around her wonderingly; the gardeners have done a very good job indeed. For having cleared the front drive, they set to work on the back gardens. She meandered her way looking at the ivy that nearly obscured the beautiful red bricks of the wall. She made a mental note to tell the gardeners to pull down the ivy.

A brick path one could discern that ran along the inside of the garden perimeter which seemed to divide the garden into four rectangles. She could make out at least as much as the gardeners have cleared out as she came across a gnarled ancient tree. She contemplated it for a long time and decided it must be an apple tree.

She would love to have cider or perhaps apple jelly. She smiled and made another mental note to tell cook to make apple jelly when she thought she heard a scrabbling noise behind. She turned to look but nothing was to be seen except the ruins of a once fine garden.

"Hello?" she called. "Anyone there?"

It was eerily silent and then a voice called, "Milady!"

Sita screamed and jumped.

"Milady," hastened the farmer's boy towards her from the kitchens. "Are you alright?"

"Oh it's you, Billy" said Sita with her hand pressed on her heart to try to slow down its racing. "What are you doing here?"

"Milady, Martha told me to tell you that the trunks are in your chambers and if it pleases milady to step upstairs."

"Oh, okay," said Sita and turned to look behind her once again. Nothing moved, not even a leaf. "Did you just come from the kitchens?"

"Yes milady," more head bobbing as he led the way back to the kitchens.

Sita followed uneasily and was glad when she entered the warm noisy kitchen with its pleasant aromas. She waved to the cook and went upstairs to her rooms.

They had a pleasant afternoon rummaging through the dresses and finally they decided on one to wear to the ball. It was an ice-blue gown that shimmered as it moved.

"Oh milady, you look positively divine in that gown," said Martha reverentially.

Sita laughed but was secretly pleased with the gown. Later she modelled it for Aunt Clara who approved and said testily, "If I only remember where I put my rings, I would give them to you Sita."

"Oh Aunt Clara," said Sita immediately. "I don't require anything. You have given me more than enough."

"Nonsense child," dismissed Aunt Clara.

The evening of the ball was as enchanting as could be made by the determined staff of Stonebridge mansion. They were besotted by Lady Sita and awed by Lord Stonebridge and were most determined that nothing would stand in the way of their happiness.

Julian stood at the bottom of the staircase awaiting the arrival of the ladies and when he perceived Sita coming down, his breath caught in his throat.

She had an innate sense of style and a smooth graceful bearing. Her heavenly body was wrapped in a clinging silk gown of shimming ice-blue that reflected the blue in her eyes.

Bringing up the rear was Aunt Clara looking most imposing clad as she was in pink and with a monstrous turban atop her head. She grinned at his thunder-struck expression and flicked a finger in his face, "Attention my boy," she said.

Julian blushed painfully and bowed to the ladies even as he led them towards the main doors awaiting the arrival of guests. They did their duty acknowledging all the local gentry who eagerly graced the ball curious as they were to see whom the Earl of Stonebridge had chosen for a bride. They had no cause for complaint.

Finally, the Earl led his fiancée in the opening

dance to the ball. Aunt Clara looked around her at the ballroom, with the supper tables excellently laid. Every detail was attended to. Beeswax candles reflected the mirrors and the ballroom flooring waxed to perfection that one could see one's reflection in it. Rococo silverware gleamed and delicate little flower bowls containing orange-flower water were artfully placed across the room and bewigged, liveried footmen stood in ready at every corner of the room.

She finally glanced at Martha who had slipped in at the door and was standing quietly behind a pillar watching the couple spin in the centre. She nodded her head and smiled at her. Martha smiled back in return and bobbed a curtsy as she silently left the room. Her little lamb was in better hands now she thought with satisfaction.

As the dance came to an end, Julian held Sita's hand and addressed the gathering, "Ladies and gentlemen, Lady Sita has honoured me by agreeing to be my wife. This ball is in her honour and a celebration of our betrothal."

The crowd clapped enthusiastically and the musicians struck the first country dance. Soon they were other partners and Julian had just finished dancing with the local vicar's wife when he looked around searching for Sita.

CHAPTER TWELVE

He saw her at the far end of the ballroom dancing in the arms of a man looking more like a pirate with a scar crisscrossing one side of his face. He wondered who it could be for he certainly didn't know. Concerned Julian moved to intercept when he noticed that they were smiling at each other and Sita was talking animatedly with him and laughing.

He stood uncertain of what to do when the dance ended and they stepped out in the balcony. Julian was about to follow them when he was summoned by aunt Clara to dance with the local squire's wife and reluctantly he shouldered the mantle of host and escorted the lady to the dance floor.

Jealousy was an uncomfortable feeling he decided and he didn't much like the idea of it. He saw Sita enter the ballroom excitedly and head straight towards Aunt Clara. She leaned down and whispered something in her ears and laugh.

Julian wondered if it was a previous lover whom she was entertaining. She was enchanting tonight and he was being a perfect cad, suspecting her of a dalliance.

He didn't get another chance to speak to her and finally, the evening came to an end. The last of the guests were seen off and the hosts stood in the foyer of the main hall catching a breath.

Julian glanced at Sita who smiled back at him with her eyes twinkling.

"Opal!" he said suddenly.

"Excuse me!" said Sita frightened.

"Your eyes they remind me of opals. I will commission a necklace tomorrow or rather today itself from the London jewellers"

"Her eyes remind you of opals?" asked Aunt Clara interestedly.

"Don't you think so aunt?" asked Julian. "Her eyes look like they contain lightning that fell from the sky during thunderstorms."

Sita blushed fiery red all over while Aunt Clara teased Julian, "Waxing poetic, my boy? Love does that to one."

Julian made to take Sita's hand when Aunt Clara said sharply "Now, no more of that Julian. You just have to wait until the banns are read and you are married. Martha, take your mistress to her room and Julian off to yours."

Julian shrugged while Sita blushed as she made her separate way to her bedchamber. Julian thought it was a pity because he wanted to ask her who that man was.

He prepared to follow her when the butler Claude cleared his throat interrupting him.

"What is it Claude?"

"The men we sent in search of Squire Grimes have come to report milord," he said.

"Excellent," said Julian stepping back down from the stairs. "Show them into the study."

Julian stepped into his study and poured himself a drink and sat down at his desk. Finally he would have information and he would ensure that the Squire paid.

"Milord!"

He looked up and saw Claude standing in the doorway and he slowly stepped aside and let the two men in who were clutching at their caps nervously.

"What information you have for me?" he asked.

"Milord, we searched the village and anyone we asked only said that the Squire left in a rage. So we followed the road South milord and there carelessly thrown by the side of the road was the body of Squire Grimes," said one man.

"Or at least what remained of him," offered the other.

"What?" exclaimed Julian shocked. "Squire Grimes is dead?"

"Yes milord."

"A grisly sight milord."

"What happened?"

"Looked like someone slit his throat, milord."

"And chopped up his privates as well."

"Good lord!" exclaimed Julian and sat back in shock. "But who?"

"Dunno, milord," said one man phlegmatically. "Looked to be a day old, the corpse that is."

"What should we do milord?" asked the other.

Julian sighed. "Take a gig and collect the corpse and give it a decent burial and we will inform whoever is next of kin of the fact. Good lord! What a mess!"

The men nodded and bowed to him and left the study.

Julian downed his drink and went up to his bedchamber. Tomorrow he would ask Sita who that man was as he fell asleep.

The next morning dawned bright and early and Julian was feeling mighty disgruntled. His beloved Sita was playing hard to get and try as he might the women in the house were ganging up on him.

They would think he was out to ravish her the way they were behaving he thought disgruntledly although it wasn't such a bad idea. He was marrying her after all and he announced the fact to the whole world.

After breakfast, he walked in the gardens sniping away the heads of flowers with his walking stick as he thought about the death of Squire Grimes and uneasily wondered what he should do about it. He did write to his secretary in London to trace this Squire fellow.

Laughter tinkled in the wind and Julian stopped entranced. Sita! He thought and hurriedly made his way towards the laughter but stopped short when he heard a male voice in laughter.

"Ah my love, I missed you," crooned Sita as she lay her head on the man's chest. "Please don't leave me and go away again."

It was the same man from last evening's ball thought Julian angrily.

"Now Sita, I am glad I have finally found you but you must accept that I have to leave."

"Unhand her sir," shouted Julian as he stepped into the little clearing where this lovely play was taking place. "I will chop off your hands if you don't unhand her now," he threatened brandishing the walking stick.

Sita screamed and threw herself in front of the man. "No, Julian. You must not."

"Stand aside, Sita. I will not let him dishonour you."

"You don't understand, Julian."

"Yes stand aside, Sita," said the amused voice. "Let's see what your fiancé is capable of."

"No-no, you must not," screamed Sita but was firmly lifted and placed aside by the man who suddenly drew a sword from his side and held it easily, point facing downwards.

Julian stood up straight and twisted the head of the walking stick and out came a sword hidden in its recesses.

"No, Julian, you must not," begged Sita.

"You love him that much my lady?" sneered Julian as he prepared to lunge at him.

"He is my brother," shouted Sita crying.

"What?" said Julian stopping in mid-lunge and his sword was harmlessly parried aside.

"Dominic, behind you!" shouted Sita and flung her dagger at a bush.

Julian saw Dominic whirl around in time to see Sita's dagger embed itself in the heart of a fellow readying to throw a dagger at him.

Three others rushed at him with swords and soon Julian and Dominic were parrying swords thrust at them. It was a short but bloody battle but they made short work of it and Julian felt his sword slide into the heart of the last one as he collapsed in front of him. He pulled his sword free and turned to look at the other man facing him with a sword dripping blood.

They locked glances but before he could say a

word, Sita rushed to him and hugged him laughing and crying at the same time, "You are safe. Thank god you are safe."

Martha bustled about and dropped a curtsy to the other man and said respectfully, "Your Grace!"

Julian cocked an eyebrow at the appellative and throwing an arm around Sita holding her close he said, "Looks like an explanation is due. Why don't we go to my study and get a drink?"

The other man nodded and they made their way through the gaggle of servants gathered in the garden watching the contretemps and hurriedly they dispersed when they saw the noble group bearing down on them.

Julian led the way to the study. He instructed Claude to pour even as he asked Martha to remain. He sent a footman to get Aunt Clara and finally he sat Sita down on the sofa and sat down beside her and elegantly gestured for the other man to sit opposite them.

Claude handed the glasses of drink and he saluted with his before downing it.

"Now perhaps an explanation is due?" he asked looking at Sita.

"Allow me," said the tall dark man standing by the fireplace with his hands folded across. "Let me paint a tale so outlandish that I fear you might not believe but it is the truth nevertheless."

"Go on," said Julian coldly. "I will reserve

judgement."

Sita started on hearing that but Julian only tightened his arm around her holding her still.

CHAPTER THIRTEEN

"It is true that Lady Sita is my sister and I am Dominic, Duke of Andover."

"The missing Duke!" started Julian surprised.

Dominic bowed ironically.

"We are the eldest of eight siblings. It was a rare love that brought mama and papa together for mama was an Indian princess."

Julian glanced at Sita and smiled, "So that explains your name."

She smiled tremulously at him.

"Mama brought as her heritage the famed Queen's Jewels. But the Rajah of Shamapur coveted them and followed her here and killed both of them in a cowardly manner."

"We had to run and escape before they killed us as well and so we all separated swearing that we will meet one day," continued Sita.

"This is all too fantastic," commented Julian.

"Nevertheless, it is true," said Aunt Clara.

They turned to look at the old lady framed at the doorway as she slowly made her way to the front of the room.

"I was there at the ball when the Bejewelled One declared Dominic as heir to the Dukedom and bestowed the Queen's Jewels upon each of her children. She sang a special song for them as well."

"You were there," repeated Sita awed at the old lady who remembered her mother and father.

"The tale of your parents love was legend as was their death, my dear," said Lady Clara gently. "It did the rounds of London for so long; for everyone was shocked."

Sita's eyes filled with tears. "That was the last I saw of my brothers and sisters. All this time I have been running and hiding."

"You will not run and hide anymore, my love," said Julian firmly.

"I am afraid it's my fault that the little incident took place in the gardens," said Dominic apologetically. "I knew they would follow me and yet when Mr Timms informed me that he was finally able to track Sita down, I couldn't resist. I had to see for myself how my little sister fared."

"Oh Dominic," said Sita as she flung herself at him and burst into tears. "Please don't leave me. Stay here."

"You know I cannot do that Sita," said Dominic gently pushing Sita away. "I will bring nothing but trouble. Besides, I have to now search for the others. I pray they are safe and sound."

"Dominic!" said Sita urgently. "There is something I must say."

"What is it?"

"I have lost the Queen's Jewel."

"What happened?" asked Dominic calmly.

"We were staying at an inn and we were attacked and Martha saved me in the nick of time but we were afraid that Martha might have killed the man in the process and so we left urgently but everything was such a chaos that day. And the Jewel was stolen from me."

She stopped the rush of words and looked helplessly at her brother.

"I am sorry," she whispered.

"It is what it is," said Dominic. "If it's destined for you it will reach you"

"I have one of the Queen's Jewels," declared Aunt Clara. Everybody started and looked at her in surprise.

"Well, don't be surprised. One day I was shopping at Rundles in London and there was some whispering about the Queen's Jewel and so I told him I will buy it from him to keep it in trust for the real owner. And here it is," she finished dramatically bringing out the Queen's Jewel and there it lay like a goose egg in the palm of her hand.

"The Opal" breathed Sita wide-eyed in wonder.

"You know, that's what sent me thinking," mused Aunt Clara as the others crowded around her admiring the Jewel in her hand. "When Julian mentioned how your eyes look like Opal, I remembered having bought one and guess where I put them?"

"Your rings Aunt Clara," exclaimed Sita noticing that her aunt's fingers were once again carrying rings. "You found them."

"I found them and the Opal because as soon as I fell ill, I removed my jewels and placed them in one of the newel posts of my bed. It has a screw top and hollowed cylinder. I found them last night just before going to bed and wanted to show them to you this morning."

"How fortunate my lady," said Dominic. "It seems that Sita has arrived at the right place for that particular Queen's Jewel belongs to her."

Everyone turned to look at Sita who smiled and gently palmed the Opal. "It is true. Mama gave it to me specially. Oh Aunt Clara I cannot thank you enough"

"Nonsense child, I did what I had to do," pooh-poohed Aunt Clara.

"And I must do what I have to do," said Dominic looking at Sita and lifting a hand to stop her protests just as she opened her mouth. "No sister. I wish you joy in your new family and may you be blessed with love and happiness."

"Thank you Dominic," said Sita shyly. "I wish you joy and happiness too"

"I doubt if that is part of my destiny," said Dominic sadly. "But before I leave, I must impress upon you the need to keep the part about your heritage quiet. Remain with the story that you are the niece of Aunt Clara and all will be well. If the Rajah's men see me turn back from here and not return they will not come near you thinking it was a false trail that led them here."

"But for how long?" protested Sita.

"Until I trace all our brothers and sisters," said Dominic firmly. "They also will be in danger if it be known that I am looking for them. So I have to do this as quietly as I possibly can and it is best for you to remain incognito for that time."

Sita nodded sadly having understood Dominic's injunction. Julian nodded in agreement to beware and shield his family and to ensure that whatever action occurred did not and could not rebound on those that they cared about, those under their protection.

"But please Dominic, won't you stay for my wedding?" pleaded Sita.

Dominic nodded and said, "I will return after three weeks in time to give you away."

"Oh, thank you, Dominic. It will be like having papa," said Sita trying hard not to cry.

"I will have a drink with Julian before I depart," announced Dominic indicating the ladies to take their leave which they did sadly.

"Thank you Martha, for looking after my little sister. She has turned into a lovely young lady I am proud to call my own. Thank you Aunt Clara for sheltering them in their time of need."

He gave them a quaint bow and kissed his sister and they curtsied to His Grace, the Duke of Andover.

Finally the room fell silent. Julian poured Dominic a drink before pouring one for himself.

"Claude's men informed me of the death of Squire Grimes," said Julian suddenly breaking the silence on an afterthought.

Dominic nodded grimly "He touched my sister, hounded her when she was alone and helpless, I castrated him and slit his throat and so no more will he prey on unprotected women."

Julian controlled his shiver as he looked into the deadened eyes of the Duke of Andover. He thought gladly that this was one facet that Sita was spared from seeing. She would not want to know the horror her brother was capable of unleashing.

"How did you know?" Julian asked tentatively.

"He was boasting of it," said Dominic simply.

They exchanged a glance and gently closed the door to a past and turned their minds to the future.

"These men who are after you," said Julian "If you require a sword by your side, know that you can count upon me."

Dominic nodded and said, "I thank you brother. I pray the need shall never arise." He downed the drink and stood up to leave. He acknowledged the hug from Julian and left by the open window through the gardens.

He turned and stood for a moment looking at the mansion. He saw Julian in his study his hand lifted in farewell, he saw his sister, Sita standing in the chamber above the study blowing him a kiss in farewell and folding her hands in Namaste.

He felt the old familiar strands of love flowing, twining, braiding and linking them to the all-inclusive power of love that he used to feel with mama and papa. Sita at least found her fairy tale ending he thought as he rode out into the night.

THE END

AFTERWORD

The idea for The Bejewelled Family Saga came upon me in 2015. But due to various personal commitments, I didn't really get around to start work on this series. I was content to merely work out the titles and the little poems that go with the Jewels and left it at that. It was only during the "Lockdown" that I turned to look at my unfinished work and was inspired to take up writing and completing the series. It was an outpouring of love and labour, a burst of excitement and creation, a waltz of characters dancing their way to tell their side of the story.

ABOUT THE AUTHOR

R. J. Kalpana

R. J. Kalpana is an Indian novelist, short story writer, a critic and a management consultant. She earned her PhD on Feminist Issues in Indian Literature. She is now branching into writing historical romance fiction.

THE BEJEWELLED FAMILY SAGA

The Bejewelled Family Saga is the story of love and loss of a family. We follow the family from the parents enchanting romance to the children's own coming of age challenges. It takes us from the palaces of India to the ducal estates of England, from the gutters of London to the high Ton of English Society. It is the story of an Indian Queen's fabled Jewels and the enemies that seek to covet it.

The Bejewelled One

It is a tale as old as time, of an enchanting romance between an Indian Queen and an English Duke. He helps her escape her enemies and takes her to the ducal estates in England. The Queen's fabled jewels are much coveted by the enemies who aren't afraid to kill on English soil.

Opals For Hope

Lady Sita is on the run and when she comes upon a Lady of the manor lying ill and unattended, she

decides to stay on and help until her nephew Lord Julian Stonebridge arrives from India and looks with suspicion upon his newest cousin. In midst of all this, trouble comes calling in the guise of the Rajah's men and her long-lost brother Dominic.

Amethysts For Love

Leila is London's most beautiful courtesan and legendary are the men at her pretty feet styled as she is as the Indian princess. Lord Richard Rivenhall is a spy in the Foreign Office and clues lead him to think that she is a traitor. Leila is not who Richard thinks she is but she has her own deadliest secrets to hide.

Emeralds For Envy

Coerced into being a jewel thief, Leonie breaks into the Devil Duke's mansion and is caught red-handed by the Devil himself. From the gutters of London she grew up innocent and as pristine as a lotus amongst pond slime and he was so disillusioned by human nature that nothing stirred his interest anymore. Would this reckless beauty bring him back from the edge of darkness before fate intrudes in the guise of her enemies?

Pearls For Innocence

Lord Spencer Huntingdon driven to purchase a commission to impress his fiancée returns from

the war a scarred cripple. Jilted, he now lives in the shadows of the Huntingdon Priory hiding his scarred face from the world warped in his aching loneliness and fear until one fateful night, a beautiful woman on the run stumbles upon him and warns him of jewel thieves. Lady Isha forced to dress up as a boy warns Lord Spencer and then stays on to cure him of a raging fever. But she doesn't stay long enough to find out if her herbs have healed his scars and his leg until they meet in the most exclusive ballroom of the Ton along with his ex-fiancee.

Sapphires For Danger

Davina becomes an unwilling witness to a race fixing racket and she rushes to inform the Marquis of Thorncourt that one of his men will soon betray him. Sylvester scorns her and so she disguises herself as a boy and trains his horses until Sylvester is forced to acknowledge the threat is real. They leave for London to discover more clues and there she meets her sister. now Duchess of Winterbourne. Davina knows Sylvester is the Ton's most eligible bachelor but will he offer her the love she desperately seeks?

Topaz For Fidelity

When wealthy heiress Lady Annbella Maybricks is importuned to marry by her odious uncle coveting her wealth, she takes matter in her own hands

and runs away and strikes a deal with a stranger at an inn. Lord Damian traveling incognito on the run since his parents death looks upon her proposition with suspicion and then decides that marrying her and taking possession of her estate Greenwoods Park is the perfect disguise until his and her enemies catch up with them for a final reckoning.

Amber For Passion

Driven to get out of her stepbrother's clutches Helen Amberfeld took the opportunity when she was staked in a game of chance. She decided that she would rather walk away with Lucian who won her than remain with her stepbrother. But their journey to her estate was fraught with peril being chased by highwaymen and kidnappers until they finally arrive at Bellaview, her inheritance only to meet with Lucian's forbidding brother, Dominic who immediately suggested marriage. Was that her only option or would she be dragged by her step-brother and forced into marriage with his friend?

Diamonds For Tears

After spending years in the glittering ballrooms of the Ton, Miranda Mellors is bored to tears by the current crop of beau. Determined to marry a man of her choice she goes where no respectable lady should, into the most exclusive gaming hell of London where she discovers she is surrounded by the

rakes of the worst order only to be rescued by the mysterious owner of the famed gaming hell. Lord Wulfric had delayed his entry into Society awaiting his brother. They meet at the Duke of Winterbourne's Chateau d' Winter for a family reunion where they are followed by their enemies who boldly attack the ladies leaving Miranda bewildered and out-of-depth amidst this bold family.

Corals For Remembrance

Caught red-handed in the arms of a notorious fortune hunter and publicly denounced by her fiancé Lady Rosalyn Anderson at Lady Whistledon's ball, Lady Rosalyn is furious with her parents and the Ton and decides to run away. She boards the ship 'Coral Lady' and finds she had just handed her virginity to the captain. Will Tristan leave the memories of his dark past behind long enough for him to embrace the present or will the return of his brother Dominic into his life be the trigger that will loosen the demons within?

Rubies For Revenge

Lady Sybila Overton is forced into an engagement with the Rajah of Shamapur. Unable to go through the farce of a marriage she contemplates jumping into the Thames when she is rescued by the Duke of Andover. The elusive Duke has come back from the dead to claim his dukedom and finally end the feud

between himself and the Rajah - to take revenge for his parent's deaths. In a world where treachery and betrayal reign, a world where greed and lust rule, Lady Sybila is trapped in a desperate web of fears, murder and intrigue. Does she and Dominic have the courage to reach out to the destiny of love that all the forces of the world cannot defeat?

BOOKS BY THIS AUTHOR

The Bejewelled One

It is a tale as old as time, of an enchanting romance between an Indian Queen and an English Duke. He helps her escape her enemies and takes her to the ducal estates in England. The Queen's fabled jewels are much coveted by the enemies who aren't afraid to kill on English soil.

Printed in Great Britain
by Amazon